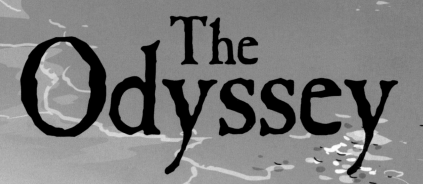

The Odyssey

Retold by Louie Stowell
from the epic tale by Homer

Illustrated by Matteo Pincelli

Reading consultant: Alison Kelly
Roehampton University

Contents

Chapter 1

Calypso's prisoner

On the island of Ogygia – home of the sea nymph Calypso – a big strong man was sitting on the beach and sobbing his heart out. His name was Odysseus, and he was a very long way from home.

Far above him, the mighty gods of
Mount Olympus were watching. Athena,
Goddess of Wisdom, turned to her father,
Zeus. He was king of all the gods; if
anyone could help Odysseus, he could.
She pointed to the tiny, ant-like human
below. "Look, Father. Poor Odysseus has
been stranded there for years. Will you
help him to escape from Calypso's island
and get home to his family?"

Zeus scowled. "Why should I help him?" he asked. "He's just a human."

"He's not just any human, Father," said Athena. "He's a hero! A clever hero, not like a lot of the blockheads out there."

"Hmm," said Zeus. "That may be true. But what about Poseidon, God of the Seas? He hates Odysseus and he'll be furious if I help him. Besides, your hero will have to escape Calypso's island by sea, so making Poseidon angry is not a good idea."

"But you're King of the Gods," Athena said, arching an eyebrow. "Your word is law. All other gods must bow to you."

Zeus grunted, obviously pleased. "That is true." He called to a young, handsome god nearby, "Hermes! Go and tell that pesky Calypso to let Odysseus go!"

Hermes saluted, scrambled into his golden winged sandals and pushed off into the empty air.

Down... down... down...

When Hermes landed on Ogygia, he found himself in a beautiful forest, surrounded by lush vegetation and the delicious smell of herbs. Somewhere close by, a scented fire was burning. And then, he saw her... Calypso.

Even though Hermes was a god, who spent his days with beautiful goddesses, he was still stunned by her loveliness.

Calypso welcomed him warmly. At least, she did until he told her why he was there...

"You want me to give up Odysseus?" Her eyes flashed with fury. "But I love him! He has lived with me for seven years."

"Against his will..." Hermes pointed out.

Calypso gave him a fiery look.

"Zeus commands you to let him go," Hermes added.

At that, Calypso sighed. "Then I must."

Calypso padded down to the beach where Odysseus sat, staring out to sea. He looked up as he heard her footsteps.

"Zeus is forcing me to let you go," Calypso said. She fluttered her eyelashes. "If you want to leave, that is..."

"I want to go," said Odysseus, quickly. "You're very beautiful, Calypso. But I want to see my wife and child and my home again. That's where I belong."

With a lovesick sigh, Calypso gave up. She helped Odysseus to build a sturdy raft, and he sailed away without a glance in her direction.

Far above Odysseus's little raft, the sea god Poseidon looked down and saw that Odysseus was free.

"So, Zeus let you go when I wasn't looking? You're not getting away that easily, little man," he muttered. He stuck his trident into the sea and stirred it up into a ferocious storm.

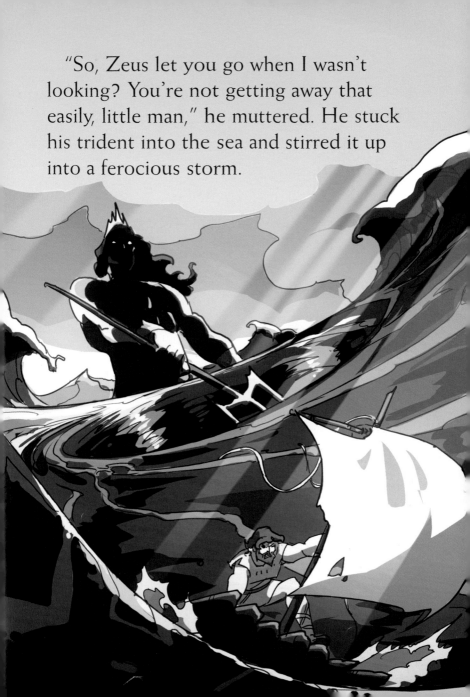

The winds and the rain lashed the little raft until it was smashed to pieces, and Odysseus was thrown into the sea. He felt himself sinking down and down into the freezing ocean. The deeper he sank, the colder it got. Soon, he knew no more.

When he came to, he found himself on a beach beside a clump of olive trees. For a horrible moment, he thought he was back where he'd started, on Ogygia.

Then he saw a pair of girls washing clothes in the river close by. *"This can't be Ogygia,"* he thought. *"I was alone with Calypso there."* He got up and called out, "Hello?"

The girls gave a squeal of shock. Odysseus bowed low. "I'm sorry if I scared you. But do you know where I might find food and shelter?"

The girls, still trembling slightly, pointed out a palace, up a hill.

As it turned out, the king and queen who lived in that palace were the perfect hosts. Without even asking who he was, they ushered him inside, gave him fresh clothes and plenty to eat and drink.

"In return for this fine hospitality," said Odysseus, "I'll tell you all a tale."

A murmur of excitement went through the court. Odysseus cleared his throat and began: "My name is Odysseus and, unfortunately for me, everything I'm about to tell you is true..."

Chapter 2

Odysseus's tale

Although you wouldn't know it to look at me, I'm a king. My kingdom is on the island of Ithaca, and I've been trying to get back there for the past seven years.

When I set sail for home, my men and I had just won a war against Troy. It took ten years and we lost many comrades. Still, twelve ships full of my men survived, and we were glad to be going home at last. At least, we *thought* we were going home...

Our journey began badly when a storm blew us off course, leaving us adrift for days. When we finally saw land, my men cheered and rushed ashore.

Unfortunately, the island was the land of the Lotus Eaters, where the fruit is so delicious, you never want to leave. After one taste, my men lost all interest in home. All they wanted was the fruit! I had to drag them back to the ship and lock them up before we could be on our way.

We sailed on. On the next island, we discovered a gigantic cave near the beach. Someone obviously lived there, so I said: "Men, let's wait here to see whose cave it is. Maybe he can give us supplies, or at least directions?"

As it turned out, that was a terrible idea. The cave was the home of a Cyclops, a one-eyed giant, and his single eye wasn't in the least pleased to see us.

As he arrived home with a herd of giant sheep, he roared at us. "Who are you?"

He rolled a huge stone over the entrance to trap us inside. "I am Polyphemus and this is my house! Why are you here?"

I spoke up. "We're weary soldiers on our way back from a war," I said. "And, as I'm *sure* you know, the great god Zeus looks kindly on those who are kind to strangers." I winked at him. "So it's probably a good idea to give us food and water..."

The Cyclops burst out laughing, spraying a shower of foul-smelling spit over us all. "Zeus? Hahahahaha! I'm not afraid of him – he's my uncle!"

With that, he plucked up two of my men in his meaty hands – and *ate* them, raw. After a swig of sheep's milk, the monster grabbed another two. Some of my men cried, "Kill him. Kill him now!"

But, looking at the huge stone blocking the door, I knew I couldn't. "We'll be trapped if he dies," I whispered to Eurylochus, my right-hand man. "But I have another idea..."

Chapter 3

A cunning plan

I gathered a few of my men in a huddle and pointed out a branch in the corner of the cave. "Sharpen that," I told them.

Then, I turned to the Cyclops, who was eyeing up my men, deciding which poor soul to eat next.

"We hardly have any food or water, but we do have some very fine wine with us," I called. "Would you like some?"

The Cyclops beamed. "Yes! Give it to me!" He grabbed the bottle and took a swig. "What's your name, stranger?"

"My name is Nobody," I said. (This was part of my plan.)

"Well, Nobody," said the Cyclops. "I shall do something nice for you, since you did this for me..."

I was about to thank him, when he went on: "Yes. I'll eat you last! Ha, ha, ha, ha!"

"Oh," I said, and I gulped. "Would you like some more wine?"

Soon, just as I had hoped, the wine made him sleepy and he began to doze, snoring like a sty full of pigs.

I gestured to my men to heat the sharpened branch in the fire. When its sharp end was white-hot, we hefted it onto our shoulders and jammed it into the Cyclops' closed eye with a sizzle.

He woke with a jolt and screamed out: "Nobody's hurting me! Help!"

Another giant who lived next door heard him and laughed. "If *nobody*'s hurting you, then stop crying, you great big baby!"

Furious and whimpering in pain, the blinded Cyclops lay back down and eventually fell asleep.

The next morning, he rolled the stone away from the cave mouth to let his sheep out to graze.

At my order, each man strapped himself quickly and quietly beneath one of the Cyclops' huge sheep. As each animal wandered out into the fields to graze, one of my men escaped into the free, fresh air.

Once outside, we let the sheep go and ran to the ship. In my triumph, I couldn't resist turning back and yelling, "I tricked you! I'm not Nobody! I'm Odysseus!"

The Cyclops howled and began to throw rocks at us – luckily, his aim was terrible. "Father! Poseidon! God of the Seas!" he cried out. "Odysseus has blinded me. Punish him! Make him suffer as I suffer!"

"Oh dear," I said to Eurylochus, as we sailed away. "Do you think telling him my real name might have been a mistake?"

Chapter 4

The bag of winds

I tried to put the Cyclops' curse out of my mind, and we sailed on peacefully enough until we reached the island of Aeolus, Keeper of the Winds.

Unlike our last host, Aeolus welcomed us kindly. We stayed at his palace for a month, feasting and telling stories.

When we left, Aeolus gave me a strange and wonderful present.

"Here," he said to me, handing me a bulging cloth bag. "This bag contains powerful winds. Let out just a few puffs if you need to change course."

I put the bag in a safe place, where my men wouldn't accidentally open it, and we went on our way.

Aeolus also sent us a steady breeze to blow us home. Before we knew it, we were close enough to Ithaca to see people walking about on the shore.

By now, I was so exhausted that I couldn't keep my eyes open, and I took a nap. I dreamed of Penelope, my wife, and Telemachus, my son, who must be almost a man now.

As I slept, some of my men pulled out the bag full of winds. They must have thought it contained treasure, because they opened it.

A mighty hurricane whipped up around us. I woke with a start and realized that my men had released all the winds at once.

We were blown back and back and back the way we had come... all the way back to Aeolus. This time, he wouldn't help us.

"The gods seem against you," he said. "I can't do anything more."

So, we set sail yet again, only this time, without the winds of Aeolus, our ships seemed to crawl through the water.

After a while, we came to an island and landed to stock up on food and water.

I spotted a girl walking along the road, and I called out to her. She told us to go and see her mother and father, the king and queen of the Laestrygones, in their palace on the hill.

"They'd be delighted to have you for supper," she said, with a smile that I didn't like all that much.

When we met the king and queen, we found out *why* they'd be so delighted – they were cannibals!

We ran for our lives, but not all of us escaped. The Laestrygones army chased us all the way to the shore and hurled rocks at us, smashing almost all of our ships and killing many of my men.

Then, they heard a woman singing. At the sound of their footsteps, she came to the door and beckoned. "Come, strangers. You look tired. Let me offer you refreshments."

The weary men went in, hungry and eager and enchanted with this kind and beautiful stranger. "Come in, come in," she sang. "I am Circe and you are welcome in my home. I have sweet wine and fresh bread, honey and olives, ready and waiting for you."

But Eurylochus stayed behind. We'd had so little good luck on our journeys that he couldn't help thinking that she was a little *too* interested in feeding them.

He peered through the window to see the men stuffing their faces with food.

As they ate, Circe brought them extra little treats and kept their cups full to overflowing. She smiled at them and they all seemed to be having a wonderful time.

Too late, the men discovered that the wine was drugged, and Eurylochus watched them slump into a deep, deep sleep. Circe waved a long, slender wand, and cried out, "Since you eat like pigs... pigs you shall be!"

Each sleeping man transformed into an oinking, snuffling, pink, wriggling pig.

Eurylochus ran all the way back to the beach and told me what he'd seen.

Telling him not to let the rest of the men out of his sight, I set off along the path in the direction of the house.

Before I'd gone half the distance, a beautiful young man in winged sandals flew down from the sky and handed me a small sprig of magic herbs.

"I am the god Hermes," he said. "Here, eat this herb. It will protect you from Circe's magic."

Before I could reply, he flew away again.

I swallowed the herbs and went on my way. At the house, I saw the tame wolves and kindly lions and wondered if they, too, had once been men.

Circe welcomed me inside, offering me food and wine. I ate and drank, just as my men had done — but I knew I was safe, thanks to Hermes.

Circe waved her wand, chuckling to herself, no doubt very pleased that she'd found another gullible idiot... but nothing happened. "Why aren't you changing?" she pouted.

"That's my business," I said, and drew my sword. "Now, change my men back."

Circe looked impressed. "It's a long time since anyone has been able to cheat my magic." She smiled softly. "Perhaps you would like to stay as my guest instead of my prisoner?"

Her eyes twinkled as she spoke, and in that instant, I began to fall in love. Or perhaps, despite the herb, I was falling under another spell. Still, I hadn't *entirely* lost my mind. "I'll only stay if you swear that you don't mean me any harm," I said. "And," I added, "reverse the spell you cast on my men!"

Circe sighed, and agreed. "I swear on all the gods that I will do you no harm." Then, she called the pigs – my men – to her and tapped each one with her wand.

The pigs began to change and grow, until my men all stood before me, looking dazed and scared.

I explained that Circe had sworn that she wouldn't hurt us, so we all decided to stay for a while. I have to admit, it was pleasant to be in a place where no one was trying to kill me or eat me, for a change.

Chapter 5

Dead men and deadly voices

After a year on Circe's island, my men grew restless, and I knew that it was time for us to leave.

"If you don't want to stay, I won't stop you," said Circe. "But, take my advice, if you want to get home in one piece, you will have to visit the land of the dead and seek the help of Tiresias, a spirit there."

I was terrified. "How can we go to the land of the dead and not die?" I asked her. "And how do we get there?"

Circe gave me a long list of instructions, as well as many warnings for our journey. "Let the North Wind carry you," she said as she waved us off in our one remaining ship. "Good luck!"

Soon, we landed on the misty shores of the land of the dead, where a sacred grove of dark trees grew.

As Circe had instructed me, I dug a little hole and poured the blood of a freshly-killed sheep into it. This was to tempt the dead out of the shadows to talk to us.

As the blood poured, shadowy spirits gathered around us. My men trembled, but I tried to keep my voice steady as I called, "Tiresias, come forward! Odysseus wants to speak to you!"

One shadowy figure drifted closer, bending to take a drink of the blood. As he began to look more solid, I saw he was an old, old man.

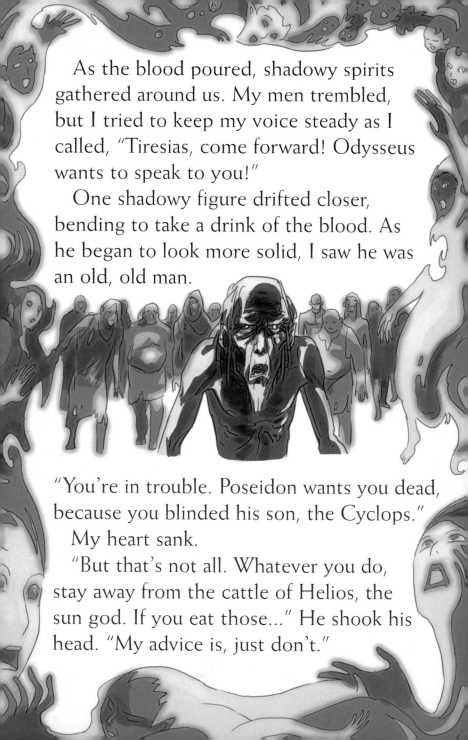

"You're in trouble. Poseidon wants you dead, because you blinded his son, the Cyclops."

My heart sank.

"But that's not all. Whatever you do, stay away from the cattle of Helios, the sun god. If you eat those..." He shook his head. "My advice is, just don't."

With the warning ringing in my ears, we left the land of the dead and sailed on. Circe had told me that another danger lay ahead: the sirens.

In case you've never heard of them, sirens are monsters with beautiful voices who lure sailors into the sea, to drown.

I gave my men wax to stopper up their ears. But I wanted to hear these voices for myself. So, I got my men to tie me firmly to the mast before we were in earshot of the sirens. Soon, I heard them...

Their voices were high and sweet, caressing my ears and urging me to come nearer, to dive into the sea... I begged my men, "Let me go... I have to go to them!"

Thankfully, they couldn't hear me through the wax stuffed in their ears. I may be the first person to hear the sirens and live. But, another danger loomed ahead. Another two, in fact.

We had to pass a narrow gap in the rocks. On one side was a whirlpool, created by the sea monster Charybdis.

On the other side was a cave where a six-headed monster lived. Her name was Scylla.

"Faster," I called to the men at the oars. "Don't get too close to the whirlpool, or we'll all be drowned!"

Just then, Scylla whipped her heads out of her cave above us. The six heads snatched up six of my men in their greedy mouths. But the rest of us were through the gap and sailing on, safe again for the moment.

Chapter 6

The cattle of the sun

We stopped for the night on an island full of golden cattle. Seeing their shining skins, I guessed that they were the cattle of the sun god, Helios, that Tiresias had warned me about.

I addressed my men in my sternest voice. "Whatever you do, do NOT eat these cattle. Don't even look at them!"

For a while, the men obeyed. But we were running low on food again, and my men began to mutter: "If we starve, we'll be dead anyway. We only have the word of a dead man for it, too."

The next day, I smelled roasting meat. My men were eating the cattle!

"Fools!" I cried. But it was too late – the damage was done. With a heavy heart, I ushered everyone back onto the ship and we set sail. What else could we do?

Moments later, the sun god Helios smashed our boat into little tiny pieces. I was the only survivor.

I found myself shipwrecked on an island, where I was taken prisoner by a magical woman named Calypso. I spent seven long years there, pining for home, until the great god Zeus sent a messenger to free me. And so here I am...

Chapter 7

Ithaca at last

As soon as Odysseus had finished his tale, he fell fast asleep in the hall of King Alcinous. The king ordered his guards to take poor Odysseus home at once. Still fast asleep, Odysseus was carried on board a ship.

When he awoke, he was on the shore of a land he thought he recognized.

With tears in his eyes, he realized: "It's Ithaca!" He kissed the ground with joy.

At that moment, a tall, beautiful woman appeared. She was wearing a breastplate that glinted in the dawn light, and had a shining helmet upon her head. It was Athena, Goddess of Wisdom, who had been watching over Odysseus all this time.

"Welcome home," she said. "But, before you can claim your kingdom, you have one last job to do. You must do it in disguise." With a wave of her hand, she transformed Odysseus into a ragged old beggar.

Odysseus gazed at his newly-wrinkled hands in shock. But he still had his wits about him. "What's the job?"

"While you've been away, your house has been full of scroungers who are eating your food and making your family's life a misery. You see, they hope that one of them can marry Penelope."

"But she *is* married!" said Odysseus.

"You've been gone a long time
– Penelope's suitors think you're dead,"
said Athena. "But I can help you get rid of
them. Go and rest in the cottage on the
hill. It belongs to Eumaeus the shepherd.
He's always been loyal to you."

Then, she disappeared.

Only one ship of sad, tired men sailed away from that island. We had no supplies, and hardly any hope left in our hearts.

Next time we landed, I was more cautious. We drew lots, and one group of men stayed at the shore with me, and the other followed Eurylochus to explore.

The scouting party soon came upon a stone house in the woods. Eurylochus told me later that outside the house were wolves and lions as meek and friendly as puppies and kittens. One lion even rolled on its back to have its tummy tickled.

Eumaeus welcomed the old stranger, offering him a place by the fire. Odysseus played the part of a feeble old beggar so well that the kindly shepherd insisted his guest should take the bed that night, while he slept outside.

The next morning, Odysseus was awoken by Athena. "I have someone to see you. But first..." She waved her hand and he felt his old and wrinkled skin become firm and young once more. "That's better," she said.

Just then, a young man appeared over the crest of the hill. He looked familiar. Very familiar.

"Telemachus! My son!" Odysseus rushed forward to hug him.

But his son flinched in shock. Odysseus's skin was still glowing from the spell. He looked more like a god than a man.

"Telemachus, I'm your father. Don't you recognize me?"

Telemachus's shock turned to joy, and he flung his arms around his father.

"It's time," said a voice from behind them. They turned to see Athena standing there. "Go and reclaim your kingdom."

She disguised him as a ragged beggar once again. "It'll give you the advantage of surprise," she said.

So, old-man Odysseus and young Telemachus walked back to town, picking up Eumaeus from his cottage on their way.

As they drew close to the city walls, a dog bounded up to Odysseus – an ancient thing, all matted hair and creaky limbs. It was Odysseus's own dog, that he'd left behind as a puppy. "Good boy, good boy!" beamed Odysseus. But his smile faded as he realized that the animal was on its last legs. "Poor boy," he whispered, bending to pat him as tears rolled down his cheeks.

But then he stood, and all the pent-up rage and bitterness of his long, long exile turned into grim determination. He *would* get his kingdom back and live happily ever after with his wife and son, if he had to kill everyone on the face of the planet to do it!

Chapter 8

The challenge

When they arrived at the palace, Odysseus found things were just as Athena had said. The great hall of the palace was full of men lazing around and eating and drinking, ordering his servants to bring them the finest things in the kitchen. Odysseus had to restrain himself from killing them all instantly.

Then he saw her: Penelope, his beloved wife. Wrinkles marked the corners of her eyes, but he thought she was the most beautiful woman he'd ever seen. He was bursting to kiss her, but he thought, *"Steady, Odysseus. You have to get rid of these suitors before you can claim your wife again."*

Penelope saw him – or rather, she saw a ragged old beggar. She called for her maid to take care of him. "Welcome, stranger. Please, rest a while." She looked around at the suitors with a wry smile. "Everyone else is making themselves at home, after all."

Odysseus followed the old maid upstairs, where she prepared a bowl of hot water to bathe his feet. As she did so, he realized he knew her – she was the maid who had taken care of him when he was a baby.

"There, that's better," she said, gently rubbing his feet and legs. All of a sudden, she stopped. "That scar on your knee looks awfully familiar. My master has one just like it..."

"Master?" she gasped. She put a hand up to his face and stroked it gently. "How..?"

Odysseus grinned and put a finger to his lips. "Shh! Everything will be revealed in time. Don't ruin my surprise!"

When Odysseus went downstairs, he saw Penelope walk into the middle of the great hall carrying a huge wooden bow. Behind her, servants came, carrying a number of axes. They set them up in a line.

"I have decided," said Penelope. "It's been long enough. I think Odysseus must be dead... so I will now marry whoever can string my husband's old bow and shoot an arrow through the line of axes."

All the suitors rushed forward, each one convinced that he would be able to do it easily. Each one tried. Each one failed.

"Let me try," said Odysseus, at last.

The suitors yelled insults, but Penelope hushed them and Odysseus took the bow. He bent it, strung it, and fired an arrow, in the time it takes to blink.

As the arrow sailed through each one of the axes, everyone in the room gasped.

"Who ARE you?" said Penelope. "There's something familiar about you."

Odysseus took her hand and kissed it, then turned to address the whole room. "I am King Odysseus!" he said. "And I'm here to claim my kingdom!"

The suitors roared in confusion and anger. Odysseus strung his bow once more and fired it into the crowd of suitors.

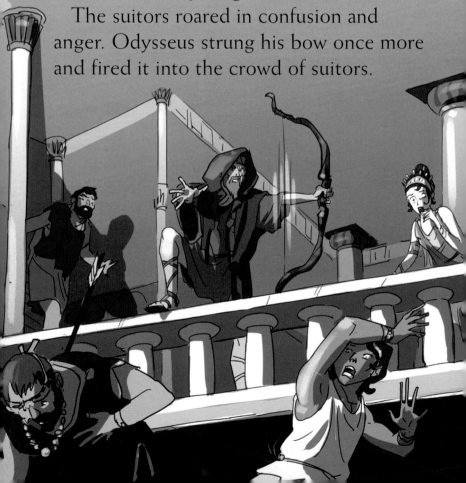

Telemachus, and Eumaeus – who was looking very surprised – backed him up, armed with spears that Telemachus had hidden earlier.

The suitors howled, "Two old men and a boy against all of us? We'll slaughter you!"

But as they attacked, they found that none of their blows hit home.

In the corner, the goddess Athena watched quietly. Each time the suitors tried to strike, she made a gesture that sent their weapons glancing off target.

The battle was over almost before it began. Odysseus was victorious. Athena touched his forehead, and the old beggar became a mighty king once more.

Penelope stared at him in shock... which turned into suspicion. "Sir. You do look like my husband. But, since you were an old man five minutes ago, I don't know who or what you really are. Still, since you passed my test, I will marry you tomorrow." Secretly, she decided to set this man another test. "I'll have my marriage bed brought down here so you can sleep in luxury tonight."

Odysseus frowned. "You can't do that! Our bed is carved out of a living tree. It can't be moved from our bedroom."

At that, Penelope burst into tears of joy. "Odysseus, it's really you!" she cried, and threw her arms around him.

For a second, Odysseus was stunned, but then he grinned, "My clever Penelope, you were testing me, weren't you?"

Penelope smiled through her tears. "Yes. But now I have my Odysseus home at last."

"Home at last," sighed Odysseus.

Homer

The Odyssey was composed nearly 3,000 years ago in Ancient Greece, by an author named Homer. It is an epic poem – a poem that tells a story about the adventures of mighty heroes and powerful gods.

Very little is known about Homer's life, but his works have been famous for thousands of years. The word 'odyssey' is now used in English to mean a long, long journey.

Homer is also the author of the Illiad, another epic poem. It tells the story of the Trojan War, between the Ancient Greeks and the Trojans. Odysseus saves the day in that story too, with a cunning trick involving a large wooden horse.

History consultant: Dr. Anne Millard
Designed by Michelle Lawrence
Series designer: Russell Punter
Series editor: Lesley Sims

First published in 2011 by Usborne Publishing Ltd., Usborne House, 83-85 Saffron Hill, London EC1N 8RT, England. www.usborne.com
Copyright © 2011 Usborne Publishing Ltd.